W9-CBG-015

CARLETON PLACE PUBLIC LIBRARY

DATE DUE

MAY 2 9 2013	
JUL 1 9 2013	
OCT 1 6 2013	

CARLETON PLACE
PUBLIC LIBRARY

To small friends the world over

STERLING CHILDREN'S BOOKS
New York

An Imprint of Sterling Publishing
387 Park Avenue South
New York, NY 10016

STERLING CHILDREN'S BOOKS and the distinctive Sterling Children's Books logo
are trademarks of Sterling Publishing Co., Inc.

Published in 2012 by Sterling Publishing Co., Inc.,
by arrangement with JB Publishing, Inc., and Ronald K. Fujikawa.
Originally published in 1988 by Random House, Inc., and © by Gyo Fujikawa
Text and illustrations © 2007 by Ronald K. Fujikawa,
Trustee of the Gyo Fujikawa Intangibles Property Trust.

All rights reserved. No part of this publication may be reproduced, stored in a retrieval system, or transmitted,
in any form or by any means, electronic, mechanical, photocopying, recording, or otherwise,
without prior written permission from the publisher.

ISBN 978-1-4027-8092-9 (hardcover)

Library of Congress Cataloging-in-Publication Data Available

Distributed in Canada by Sterling Publishing
c/o Canadian Manda Group, 165 Dufferin Street
Toronto, Ontario, Canada M6K 3H6
Distributed in the United Kingdom by GMC Distribution Services
Castle Place, 166 High Street, Lewes, East Sussex, England BN7 1XU
Distributed in Australia by Capricorn Link (Australia) Pty. Ltd.
P.O. Box 704, Windsor, NSW 2756, Australia

For information about custom editions, special sales, and premium and corporate purchases,
please contact Sterling Special Sales at 800-805-5489 or specialsales@sterlingpublishing.com.

Printed in China
Lot #:
2 4 6 8 10 9 7 5 3 1
06/12

www.sterlingpublishing.com/kids

Are You My Friend Today?

GYO FUJIKAWA

STERLING CHILDREN'S BOOKS
New York

CARLETON PLACE
PUBLIC LIBRARY

HI! ARE YOU MY FRIEND TODAY?

Let's play. Let's talk.
Let's go find the other kids.
Maybe we can all play together. . . .

WE ARE FRIENDS

Here we are, all good friends!
We spend our days together
having lots of fun.

We are going to catch some fish.

We like
to share.

Watch out,
Mr. Squirrel,
here we come!

Time to smell
the flowers.

Can we talk?

Up we go!

Up!
Down!
Up
and
down!

Down we go!

Glub, glub,
join me for a swim!

Running barefoot feels s-o-o-o good!

We are taking
the children for a walk.

Come on,
let's splash!

Hi, bird! Wouldn't you like to swing with me?

Tra-la-la, and la!

Look out below!

PLAY DAY

Big treats and little treats
make us feel so good inside.
What makes you feel wonderful?

I love a picnic
in the backyard.

OUR MONSTER

Away we go,
chasing our gigantic monster.
We're not afraid of him.
We love him.
Because, you see,
he's just pretend.
Our monster is a dinosaur
and very ancient.
He's at least
a zillion years old!

IT'S A BAD DAY

When you fall out of bed
first thing in the morning,
it's a bad day!

Or if you step on your dog's tail
(by mistake, of course) . . .

When you spill ice cream
on your brand-new dress . . .

When you bat a ball
and hurt your best friend
on the head . . .
it's a bad day.

If you stub your toe
on a stupid old rock . . .

When you slip
on a banana peel
and look silly! . . .

When you get mixed up
in a big argument . . .
it's a very bad day!

Oh, well,
there's always tomorrow. . . .
I know it'll be a very good day!

SCHOOL TIME

Mustn't be late for school!
It's time for learning
and time for playing—
lots of playing!

CARLETON PLACE
PUBLIC LIBRARY

MAKE-BELIEVE ZOO

Come and look for us
in our make-believe zoo.
We are creatures of the wild,
and we are waiting for you!

So come and visit us.
Who knows—
maybe you, too,
can be a bird or a beast
in our make-believe zoo.

HERE COMES THE MAILMAN

Guess what?
We are making our
own cards this year!

After Mama writes the addresses
on the envelopes, we'll put
the stamps on them.

Next we run to the mailbox
and send them to friends
far and near.

Then, before you know it,
here comes the mailman and
he has something for us!

Look! Look!
He brought lots and lots
of cards from all our friends,
wishing us happy holidays!

Anything for us?

DEEP FEELINGS

Everybody has all kinds of feelings,
not just good feelings
but bad feelings, too.
Lonely feelings
and sad feelings,
Angry feelings
and friendly feelings.
Disappointed feelings
and stuck-up feelings.
And there are unhappy feelings
as well as the best—
happy feelings!

Sprinkle, sprinkle,
come my way.
I would love to
soak all day!

I'm sorry . . .

Drizzle, drizzle, go away,
must you spoil our game today?

I don't like you!

Who cares?

My puppy
ran away!

You're not our
friend today!

See! We're good friends again!

DOING IT YOUR WAY

There comes a time when
you must do things
all by yourself
in your own way.

I can walk!

Isn't my hair
just gorgeous?

I'm ready to go!
How do I look?

Teeth, teeth,
here I come!

Why does Johnny think I need a bath?

My brother likes to
sleep in the doghouse.
How come?

But I like
my shoes on this way.

How did I do that?

I'm the best
sandwich maker in the
whole wide world!

Here, kitty,
kitty, kitty!

ALL YEAR LONG

January

February

May

June

September

October

March

April

July

August

November

December

A MYSTERY

Teddy bear is missing!
All day long we search
high and low for him.
Finally we see him,
perched among the leaves,
way, way up in the treetop.
Now the big question is,
how did he get up there?
It's a mystery!

After all, Teddy can't climb
like a real live bear.

But there he is in the treetop.
Somebody or something
got him there. Who?

Maybe the wind blew him up there.

Maybe one of us put him in the tree.

Not me.

Not me.

Not me.

Not me.

Meow.

Tweet.

Chirp.

Woof.

Wa-a-a-a.

Squeak.

Cluck.

The next morning we run to the tree, and guess what!
There is Teddy under the tree, sitting on the ground!

Now there are two mysteries.
How did Teddy get
up in the tree
and how did he
get down?

Do you know?

*For the answer, turn
the book upside down.*

BY MYSELF

Sometimes,
for no reason
in particular,
I climb a tree.
I just like to sit
up there
by myself
and think a whole lot
about nothing
much at all.

A VERY SPECIAL FRIENDSHIP

I have a friend,
a secret friend.
Nobody knows my friend
but me.
Nobody can see my friend
but me.
How I love
my very own,
my special,
my secret friend!

PET PARADE

Let's have a parade, everybody!
Let's show off our pets.
Ever-loving, ever-faithful,
they deserve their own
special parade.
Don't you agree?
Let's show the world
we love our pets
as much as they love us.
So join the parade,
everybody!
And shout to the skies,
"Hooray for P-E-T-S!"

THE BIRTHDAY PARTY

Yummy, yummy, yummy!
Today is my birthday!
All my friends have come
to help me eat
this great big, beautiful
birthday cake!
Yummy, yummy, yummy!

SLEEPOVER TIME

Look at us! Shouting and laughing,
we jump up and down! What fun!

Then, oh so tuckered out, we plop down to sleep
and dream of happy tomorrows!

SO LONG FOR NOW

Let's play again tomorrow.
Remember, we're friends
forever and ever!